Style Queen

Passion for Fashion

With thanks to Lucy Courtenay

First published in Great Britain by HarperCollins Children's Books in 2008.
HarperCollins Children's Books is a division of HarperCollinsPublishers Ltd.
77-85 Fulham Palace Road, Hammersmith, London, W6 8JB.

1

Text copyright © Coleen McLoughlin 2008
Illustrations by Nellie Ryan/EyeCandy and
Nicola Taylor NB Illustration 2008

ISBN-13 978-0-00-727739-1
ISBN-10 0-00-727739-3

Printed and bound in England by Clays Ltd, St Ives plc

One

Striking a pose, I winked at my reflection. A glittery eye winked back at me.

"Now *that's* a great look," I said to myself, pleased with the result. Not too much, just enough. Coleen, Queen of the Glitter Scene!

I turned up the radio and closed my eyes.

The music pumped and the glitterballs spun, dappling the dance floor with light. The girl flung back her long brown hair and swayed to the music. She could hear the whispers of the other dancers. Who

5

was this mysterious beauty? Who did her make-up? And where did she get that fabulous outfit?

"Coleen!" my mum shouted up the stairs. "I hope you're putting on your uniform! The bus goes in ten minutes!"

The dance scene fizzled away. I opened my eyes with a sigh and stared at my bedroom. It was Monday morning, and my uniform was still lying on the floor where I'd left it on Friday afternoon.

OK, so my excuse was this. Friday afternoon means one thing – total style for the whole weekend! I can't wait to get out of the whole grey and blue vibe that is school uniform, open my wardrobe and choose something fantastic. And if my uniform stays on the floor – well, too bad.

"Coleen!" Mum shouted again. "The bus!"

Quick as a flash I pulled on my stuff. After tying my tie in the funky new knot I'd perfected last week

(very skinny and tight), I slid down the banister, nearly trod on Rascal our dog and raced into the kitchen. With a quick one-two, I flipped two pieces of bread into the toaster, pulled the juice from the fridge and swigged.

"Urgh," said my little sister Em from the other side of the table, wrinkling her freckly nose at me. "You're gross, Coleen. Pour the juice into a glass, why don't you?"

Em's only seven. She can be quite cute, but has this annoying way of winding me up. As normal, her school shirt was hanging out of her skirt and she already had jam on her sweatshirt. You could vacuum Em twice a day and she'd still look a scruff. How could two sisters be so different?

"What is that on your eyelids?" Dad asked, halfway through sloshing his tea down his throat.

Oops. Make-up and school uniform is a big

7

no-no. I try to be subtle, but I guess the glitter may have been a step too far.

"It's just a bit..." I began.

"Upstairs and take it off," Mum said wearily. "The bus had better be late this morning, is all I can say."

I guess Coleen, Queen of the Glitter Scene would have to wait till I got in from school this afternoon.

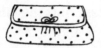

So, this is me. Petite, brown hair, brown eyes. Sometimes I wish I was taller, but they say the best things come in small packages. My nose is cute, even if I say so myself. And I love playing around with clothes.

"Coleen always has something funky going on." That's what my best friend Mel would say. She and I have different tastes – some of her stuff is way too weird for me – but we know what looks hot and

what does not. She's lucky, because bright colours look brilliant on her dark skin.

"I wish I looked like you guys." That's my other best friend Lucy, by the way. I'm not boasting – she really says dumb stuff like that. I wish she wouldn't. She's completely cute, in a blonde, blue-eyed kind of way. It's just she doesn't know it. She plays it safe, fashion-wise. Beats me why. With her long legs and brilliant voice, she could be the ultimate rock chick.

The bus, amazingly, *was* late. Mel and Lucy had already got our usual seats.

"Nice pink eyelids, Coleen," Mel said with a giggle. "Not."

My eyelids were red-raw. That's what comes of scrubbing off eyeshadow with a wet flannel in two seconds flat.

"How's things, guys?" I asked, flopping down next to Lucy.

"Ben has a zit this morning," Lucy told me. "It was really funny. He was acting like a big girl – totally gutted!"

My heart started bouncing around my stomach like a beach ball. It does that whenever Lucy's brother gets mentioned. I couldn't help gazing over where Ben was sitting with his mates Dave Sheekey and Ali Grover, a bit further down the bus. I could only see the back of his head and his gorgeous wide shoulders, but maybe – given the zit and all – it wasn't such a bad thing that I couldn't see his face. Plus I always blush when he looks at me. Gazing into your crush's eyes is all very well, but not when the side effects include beetroot cheeks.

"Your brother is still a complete love god," I sighed.

"Dream on, Coleen," Mel snorted. "Like Lu's big brother will ever take a Year Eight seriously!"

Mel was right. Ben Hanratty was Year Ten, and way out of my league. But hey, a Glitter Queen

10

should aim for the stars, right? I closed my eyes, partly because I didn't want to see Dave Sheekey sticking his finger up his nose in the seat opposite Ben, and partly because bus-time was dream-time.

She was back on the dance floor. The music was getting seriously funky. She felt like she could dance forever! The gorgeous little skirt she'd customised was spinning out as she moved, its sequins catching the reflections from the glitterballs. She opened her eyes and noticed the tall blond boy watching her from across the room. She smiled and beckoned him over...

"Earth to Coleen," Mel hissed. "Tickling the chin of some invisible cat isn't a good look. Especially when it's pointing at a Certain Someone?"

I opened my eyes. My finger was beckoning for real. Even worse, it was beckoning in the direction of Dave Sheekey, whose mouth was wide open as he gawped at me.

The bus snorted and juddered to a halt outside school. Blushing bright red, I ran for the doors with Mel and Lucy howling with laughter behind me. Not a great way to start the week.

The playground at Hartley High was awash with blue and grey as we walked through the school gates.

"It's so depressing," I said, looking around. "How are our young minds supposed to develop with no colour or style in our daily lives?"

"We make do with what we have," Mel said. "You have your choked-chicken tie thing going on, and I've got my kipper." She fiddled with the fattest tie knot I'd ever seen. It looked pretty retro. "See?" she said. "We're individuals already."

"I tried your skinny knot this morning, Coleen," Lucy said as we pushed through the double doors. "I

nearly strangled myself with my tie. Ben had to cut it off and lend me his spare. I don't know what I'm going to tell Mum."

Me and Mel burst out laughing, and the three of us linked arms and headed down the corridor to our classroom.

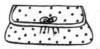

First off was drama. Drama is my favourite class. Miss O'Neill teaches us, with the help of her assistant Miss Rodriguez. Miss O'Neill is great. Her clothes, however, are not. Today's outfit was a right show. A mint-green and mud-brown swirly combo that did nothing for her complexion. Not that I'd ever dream of saying anything to her. Teachers can't help it, can they?

"Push the desks across the room please," said Miss O'Neill, clapping her hands to get our attention. "We need plenty of space today."

"Plenty of space to get away from that minging dress, you mean," came a drawling voice near me.

Summer Collins was standing in a huddle with her two saddo mates, Hannah Davies and Shona Mackinnon. They were all looking sideways at Miss O'Neill and giggling. Miss O'Neill's cheeks went pink, although she was pretending that she hadn't heard anything.

"The pattern's practically burning my eyes out of my head," Summer continued.

I couldn't help myself.

"Shame you're not standing closer then, Summer," I said in a loud voice.

Me and Summer Collins aren't exactly best mates. With her silver-blonde hair and tiny waist, Summer Collins reminds me of a doll my dog once ate. *After* he'd eaten it.

"So, Coleen," Summer purred, narrowing her eyes at me, "are you telling me you *like* Miss O'Neill's outfit?"

14

She said this so loud that even Miss O'Neill couldn't pretend not to have heard anything. How was I going to get out of this one? If I said I liked it, Summer would never let me forget it. If I said I hated it, Miss O'Neill would be upset.

Panicking slightly, I stared at Summer. My first thought was: heLLO? Summer Collins gets to wear eye make-up at school and I don't? How unfair was that? My second thought was that she'd done something really freaky to her hair, so it was poker-straight at the sides and had this weird poodle puff bit at the front. I had a flash of inspiration.

"And are *you* telling *me* you did your hair like that on purpose?" I said.

The class shouted with laughter. Summer Collins turned purple with fury. And believe me, purple clashes with green eyeshadow in a big way.

15

When the class had settled down – and Summer had got bored of shooting evils at me – Miss O'Neill put on her Announcement Face.

"I have some exciting news regarding our end-of-term project," she said. "From all your great suggestions we've decided that this year, Hartley High's Year Eight drama pupils will put on a fashion show, modelling clothes from local boutiques that will then be auctioned for charity."

I clutched at Mel's arm, dizzy with excitement. Had Miss O'Neill really just said my favourite F word? My dream engine went into hyperdrive.

The lights blazed down on the catwalk as the music began. Gorgeously dressed actresses and fashion editors sat on the front row with their pens poised over their notebooks. It was Coleen's first fashion show, and everyone was desperate for a glimpse of her work. There had been rumours for months. Coleen would be

experimental. She would be wild. She would break all fashion conventions. Vogue *was holding their front page!*

"Students will all have a chance to take part. There will be plenty of different roles," Miss O'Neill continued. "I want you all to think about what part you want to play in this event, and then stand in groups. Models over here in the middle of the room. Set designers by the door. Musicians here by the window with Miss Rodriguez, and all other volunteers by the whiteboard."

"Come on!" I said, grabbing Mel and Lucy's hands and tugging them over to the middle of the room. "Let's do the modelling!"

"Hold on, Coleen," Lucy protested. "I don't want to be a model!"

"You don't?" I said, stopping mid-tug. "So, what do you want to do?"

Lucy blushed. "Sing, I guess," she said.

17

As I've mentioned before, Lucy has a great voice. When she sings in front of us, she can be funky or sweet or sad. She can do all of it. And it's like she forgets to be shy when she's into the music.

"I'm so stupid," I said, whacking myself on the forehead. "Of course you have to sing, Lucy."

Lucy smiled, and ran across the room to where a small group of hopefuls were gathering by the window.

"You'll do modelling, won't you Mel?" I said pleadingly.

"You bet!" Mel grinned, and high-fived me. "Lemme at it, girlfriend!"

Two

No prizes for guessing who else was up for modelling. Our very own fashion victim, Summer Poodle-Hair Collins.

Summer's dad owns a boutique in Hartley which is full of big-name labels. Summer's *totally* into labels. If it's a brand you've heard of, Summer will wear it. Even if it's the most disgusting thing you've ever seen. How sad is that?

"Right," said Miss O'Neill. "You all want to be models? Let's see you strut your stuff down this space here in the middle of the room."

"I'll go first, Miss!" Summer said eagerly.

I nearly died laughing as Summer started prancing up and down, pouting and tossing her hair from side to side.

"She looks like a horse," Mel spluttered. She put on a fake race-announcer's voice. "And here comes Summer Collins, cantering up the inside. Someone ought to have plaited her mane. It must be nearly impossible to see out. Whoops! There goes a fence post!"

I thought I was going to explode, I was laughing so hard.

"Thanks, Summer," said Miss O'Neill, making a note on her clipboard. "You'll do."

My jaw dropped. I couldn't believe that Miss O'Neill had picked Summer after that rubbish performance.

"She's hardly going to say no to Summer, is she?" Mel pointed out in a low voice. "Not if she wants

Summer's dad to put some clothes in the show—"

"Coleen?" Miss O'Neill said. "You're next."

"You're not having her, are you, Miss?" Summer said at once. "She's too short to be a model."

I swear, if Mel hadn't held on to my arm, Summer would have been a large blonde splat on the floor.

"Everyone gets a chance, Summer," said Miss O'Neill firmly.

I held my head up and put one hand on my hip. Imagining myself in a pair of gorgeous high heels and a floaty chiffon gown, I started walking. All the magazines say that models walk like they're on a tightrope, putting one foot in front of the other. It's a great way of moving, and makes your hips sway like crazy. In my mind I could hear the crowds cheering and the music pumping. I could also hear Summer sniggering, but I ignored that. I just pictured her as a horse with a bridle around her head and kept going.

"Great," said Miss O'Neill, ticking her clipboard.

"I can do it?" I said, hardly daring to believe my luck. "Really, Miss?"

"Yes, really." Miss O'Neill smiled. "Mel? You're next."

Choirs of angels were singing in my head. I was going to be a model and get to wear some super-cool clothes! I stood and grinned as Mel grooved down the imaginary catwalk, fluttering her arms at her sides like a little bird.

"Terrific," said Miss O'Neill, as Summer and her mates groaned pathetically.

"I'm in!" Lucy squealed, running up to us all pink and breathless. "Miss Rodriguez said I was great! There's going to be a band with backing singers, and I'm one of them!"

"And Mel and me are models!" I yelled back delightedly.

This fashion show was going to be the event of the decade!

It was pretty hard to concentrate on anything else for the rest of the day. Maths passed in a blur. The only thing I remember about it was Mr Hughes telling me off for sketching dresses in the margin of my maths book. (Hello? Working out the proportions of bust to waist to hips is *totally* about fractions.)

It's not exactly a secret, but I've always wanted to work in fashion – not necessarily as a model, more on the design side. To create something original for someone to wear, that will make that someone feel a million dollars – that would be *serious* job satisfaction.

"Mum!" I yelled, running through the front door at full speed after school that afternoon. "Dad! Guess what!"

Dad put his head round the living-room door. "Let me see," he said, doing one of his comedy frowns. "You've invented a device that brushes your teeth and your hair at the same time?"

Dad always says stupid stuff like that. But right now I was too excited to wind him up about it. "I'm going to be a model," I said happily.

"I thought models had to be about ten feet tall," said Dad in surprise. "*And* be older than twelve. You're neither of those things, Coleen."

I groaned. "Not like a proper *Vogue* model, Dad. A model in our school fashion show!"

"Who's going to be a model?" said Mum, coming in the front door with Em.

"Me," said Dad. He struck a stupid pose in the hallway. "I've always thought I had the nose for it."

I fell over my words in my eagerness to tell Mum and Em my news.

"Fashion," Em groaned, like it was the most boring subject in the world. She took off her crumpled jacket

24

and slung it over the end of the stairs. It immediately slithered off and landed in a heap on the carpet.

"Thinking a bit about fashion wouldn't kill you, Em," I said, picking up her jacket and twirling it between my fingers. "You might learn that the dishcloth jacket is not a good look."

"That's terrific, Coleen," said Mum warmly, putting her arm around me. "Well done. So what are you wearing?"

"There's loads of stuff to do before we know that, Mum," I said as we all went into the kitchen together. "We've got to work out a theme for the show, and write to all the boutiques in town to see if they'll take part. Then there's set design and music and scripts to write and learn. It's not just about the clothes."

"Scripts?" said Dad. "Since when do models talk?"

"Each section has to be introduced," I said. "Our homework is to come up with a theme, and then argue it in front of the class next week. I've been thinking about it all day and I've come up with the best theme ever. I hope Miss O'Neill chooses it."

"What is your fashion theme?" Em asked, doing silly quotey fingers around the "F" word.

Em should know by now that asking me to talk about fashion is always a mistake. You want me to talk? I'll talk. And talk and talk and talk until your ears are ringing. And then I'll talk some more.

"Time," I said grandly.

"That's a pretty big theme, Coleen…" Mum started.

"Dawn, morning, afternoon, dusk, evening, night," I rushed on. "It's perfect, and dead flexible. We can have misty-type dresses for dawn, maybe some sunrise colours for morning. Afternoon can be cool summer outfits in the blues of the summer sky. Dusk can be all moths and that."

"Moths and that," Dad repeated.

"Fluttery grey and black cobwebby stuff," I explained.

"Plenty of that in the corners of your bedroom ceiling, Coleen," Mum murmured from behind her cup of tea.

"Evening will be all glitter and sequins, and night could be…" I stopped. I hadn't exactly worked out *night*.

"Duvets?" Dad suggested.

"Da… ad!" I wailed, pushing him as Mum and Em started laughing. "You never take me seriously!"

"Believe me, Col," said Dad with a grin, "I do."

He gathered me in and kissed me on the top of my head.

It's hard to stay mad at him when he does that.

"Whatever you come up with," Dad said as he released me, "we'll all be in the front row of this fashion show, cheering you on. But promise me something."

He looked so serious that I felt worried for a moment. "What?" I asked.

Dad's eyes twinkled. "Promise you won't forget your poor old dad when you get famous."

I laughed, relieved. "Don't be daft," I said. "But you know what I'd really like?"

"A palace with a garden full of cantering white ponies," said Dad promptly.

Em giggled.

"I'd really like to design the clothes as well as model them," I said in a rush. "That would be…" I stopped because I couldn't think of a word gorgeous enough.

"I think you might actually explode with excitement if you did that," said Dad. "So maybe it's not such a good idea. I don't fancy sweeping up the bits."

"Gross, Dad!" Em squealed.

"Who's for a chocolate biscuit?" Mum said, flipping the kettle on for another cup of tea and reaching into the cupboard to take out the biscuit barrel.

28

"Me!" Em and I both shouted at the same time, pouncing on the tin.

"I don't think so, Col," said Em cheekily, snatching my biscuit and stuffing her face with it. "Chocolate is *sooo* bad for a model's figure…"

That night, my dreams were full of rainbow silks and sequinned ribbons. For once, I couldn't wait to pull on my uniform and run for the bus.

A huge black four-by-four roared up the road past me, choking me with the stink of petrol fumes. Coughing, I looked up to see Summer Collins' stupid face grinning at me out of the tinted back window. Summer's dad always drove her to school, like maybe his baby's legs weren't up to running for the bus like the rest of us.

What if Summer Collins gets to model all the cool

stuff in the show and you get something tacky? a sneaky little voice whispered in my mind.

Coleen, I said firmly to myself, drowning out the sneaky voice, *when it comes down to it, you will get something great to wear. And even if you don't, you'll work your special magic and make it look so hot that the catwalk will sizzle!*

Feeling better for my little pep talk, I decided to try out my model walk the last few yards to the bus stop. Walking with a wiggle really makes you feel good. Except when you trip over a Coke can and land flat on your face at the last minute, just as the bus pulls into the stop and half of your school laughs themselves sick out of the windows. That stinks.

From his usual seat opposite Ben, Dave Sheekey cheered as I sat down next to Lucy and Mel and tried to sort out my bruised knee and injured pride.

"Don't worry about him," said Lucy comfortingly.

30

"He's an idiot. I don't know what my brother sees in him."

I took several deep breaths and imagined Dave Sheekey wearing a really bad pair of pants and nothing else. It cheered me up immediately.

Mel's next words, however, brought me flat to the pavement with my nose inches from that Coke can again.

"Mum says I can't do the modelling," she said, staring at her knees.

"WHAT?" I screeched, horrified. Lucy put a comforting arm around Mel's shoulders. "But *why*?"

"She says modelling 'objectifies young girls', if you want her exact words," Mel sighed.

"But that's crazy!" I spluttered. "Couldn't you persuade her to let you do it, just this once?"

"You know what my mum's like," said Mel. "Once she has an idea in her head, she sticks to it like gum."

I gawped at my best mate. This was awful! This was *worse* than awful!

"It won't be the same if you aren't modelling in the show too," I gasped. "There must be some way of persuading her—"

"Believe me," Mel interrupted me sadly, "there isn't. And talking about it isn't helping, OK? Mum won't let me model, and that's that. Can we talk about something else now?"

Three

Gutted just doesn't come near how bad I felt for Mel. She hardly said a word during PE that morning. Given that you can't usually shut Mel up, that was extremely weird. Every time me or Lucy asked her anxiously if she was OK, she muttered "Fine" and rushed off to the next piece of gym equipment like her shorts were on fire. It was like she didn't even want to be near us, because we were going to be in the fashion show and she wasn't.

"We have to do something, Lu," I said urgently as we lined up at the climbing wall.

"I know," said Lucy, biting her lip. "It's not normal seeing Mel so sad."

"What if we wrote her mum a letter?" I said.

Lucy raised her eyebrows. "Behind Mel's back? No way."

Lucy was right. I tried again.

"We have to talk to Mel's mum ourselves then, and see if we can make her change her mind," I said. "Can we go over after school this week?" I was struck by a brainwave. "A sleepover!" I said eagerly. "That'll give us plenty of time to talk Mel's mum round!"

"Great idea," said Lucy. "But you should be asking Mel, not me."

Mel walked past, her head bowed.

"Mel..." I started.

34

"Later, Coleen, yeah?" Mel said, not looking at me as she ran towards the tumbling mats.

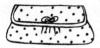

Mel couldn't avoid us forever. Lucy and I perfected our plan in time for break. And then we cornered her by the snack machine.

"Please don't start," Mel begged as I opened my mouth. "Don't you think I've been going crazy about this? You're not helping, Coleen – honest you're not. Mum won't change her mind!"

"Quit being such a wuss," I snapped. I was getting quite angry now. "Come on, Mel! This isn't like you. You're rolling over before the fight's even begun! Lucy and I have a plan. We just want you to listen, OK?"

"Like there's a choice," Mel muttered.

She didn't look like she was going to break into a run, so Lucy and I grabbed her, steered her towards a chair and sat down on either side of her, like prison guards or something.

"Why don't we have a sleepover at yours this weekend?" I began.

"We could put on a mini catwalk show for your mum," Lucy said, watching Mel nervously.

"I'll bring round some great accessories, and we'll all dress up and have a fab time," I said. "We'll show your mum how fun a catwalk show can really be."

"A sleepover?" said Mel slowly. "We haven't had one of those in ages."

Lucy and I looked at each other in excitement. Mel liked our plan!

"It'll be totally brilliant," I said, feeling enthusiastic all over. "Lucy will do the soundtrack. We might even get your mum to dress up in something too!"

"Mum does have some pretty cool outfits," Mel said. "She's kept loads of stuff from the eighties in the back

36

of her wardrobe. She might even let us borrow some."

"Oh Mel," I said happily, pulling my friend into a big squashy hug. "It's so great to see you smiling again."

"And even if your mum doesn't change her mind about the school fashion show, we'll still have a great time," Lucy added.

Mel had her old positive face on again. "Who knows what Mum'll say by the time we've finished?" she said mischievously. "Pigs *can* fly – sometimes. Erm... maybe?"

Somehow, the rest of the week zoomed by. Em had an after-school football match on the Wednesday that we all went along to watch. Then I had to walk Rascal after tea and believe me, I did some walking. I was literally dragged to the park on my knees. Then Nan came over for tea on the Thursday. Finally, I was so busy planning which accessories I was going to take for Friday's sleepover at Mel's that I didn't even rise to Em's teasing about how I might end up wearing hideous purple dungarees at the school fashion show.

I have a billion and one accessories. They drive Mum mad, because most of the time they are scattered around the house. You know – a scarf draped over the post at the bottom of the stairs, an earring under the settee – that kind of thing. But accessories are brilliant – and they're cheap, too. You can make the same old tee look totally different: dress it up one day with a red patent belt, then dress it down the next with a bunch of funky badges. Ta-da!

By the time Friday came, I had whittled my accessory selection down to four boxes. Then, remembering that I was going straight to Mel's after school that day and would have to carry everything on the bus, I reluctantly cut it down to an extra

rucksack and a carrier bag. But hey – those two bags carried some serious fashion power!

Mel and Lucy helped me carry everything from the bus stop on Friday afternoon, all the way up the stairs to Mel's place on the third floor, along with my rucksack of pyjamas and clean clothes for the next day. By the time we reached number thirty-six, I was feeling quite glad that I hadn't brought four boxes after all.

I like Mel's place. Her mum has painted it bright colours, and there are gauzy scarves hanging over all the lamps that make you feel like you are in Aladdin's cave or something. Her mum has a thing about elephants too. They are everywhere. Little ones standing on the window sills. Big ones printed on the cushions. There's pictures of elephants on the walls too, and – get this – even an elephant-shaped sponge in the bathroom!

"OK," said Mel. "Let's get ourselves a drink first. What would you like?" She walked into the kitchen and opened the fridge door. "Looks like we've got orange juice, or there's Coke too."

"Er, Coke for me," I said, smiling as the Palmers' cat, Tiggy, jumped on to the work surface and haughtily arched her back into a stretch.

"Oh Tigs, you know you're not meant to be up there," Mel groaned.

"Don't worry," I laughed, stroking Tiggy's back and tickling him behind the ears. "I've got him." And grabbing the little ginger cat tight, I followed Mel and Lucy down the corridor into Mel's bedroom.

"So Coleen," said Mel as she slumped down on to the bed, "what have you got for us?"

"Well, why don't you take Tigs," I said, handing the cat over to Lucy and grabbing what I'd brought, "and I'll show you. You are going to totally freak when you see what I've got."

I tipped out my stuff on to the bed. Mel and Lucy

pounced on my bright, twinkling collection of goodies.

"I love these," Mel said, twirling around with a pair of long blue glass earrings. "How do they look?"

"They'll look brilliant when we've done your hair," I said. "Do you think your mum would lend us some of her stuff for our show?"

Mel looked nervous. "I haven't really mentioned the catwalk thing to her yet," she said.

Me and Lucy goggled at our mate.

"Your mum doesn't know?" I repeated.

Mel pleated her bedcover between her fingers. "She's been really tired lately, and she's really dead set against models and catwalks. I thought maybe – we could do it as a surprise?"

"Looks like we'll have to," I said. Suddenly, I was feeling as nervous as Mel looked. What if Mrs Palmer got really mad at us?

The next minute, I forgot my worries as Mel took

us down the hall to her mum's bedroom and went to her wardrobe. "Ta-da!" she announced as she pulled open the door.

I almost fell over. The cupboard was totally crammed with colour. A yellow jacket. An emerald green dress. Red and blue and white printed blouses, and shimmery purple and blue trousers.

"The eighties are *so* in right now!" I said, grabbing an orange jersey dress off the rail and holding it up against myself. I knew immediately that the long blue glass earrings would go perfectly!

"Mum's getting back at five-thirty today," said Mel as Lucy tried on a pair of bright blue skinny trousers. "Why don't we get everything ready and surprise her with the show as soon as she comes through the door?"

We spent the next hour working out which outfits to choose – there were so many fantastic things. In

the end, my accessory selection made the choices for us. My peacock-feather necklace screamed to go with the emerald green dress. The orange jersey dress got the blue earrings, and the yellow jacket looked super-cool with a thick black patent belt around the middle.

Lucy rushed around the living room, getting everything ready for the show and choosing the music. She chose something with a soft, pulsing beat that perfectly matched a steady model wiggle. Then we all got changed.

We were just putting the last layer of lip gloss on when we heard keys in the front door. We gulped and looked at each other. Was this really going to work?

"It's now or never," Mel muttered, and she pushed me through the bedroom door.

We teetered down the corridor in our high heels and peeped around the corner as Mel's mum came in. She looked tired, and her shapeless black coat made me think of an old horse blanket.

"Hi, Mum!" said Mel in an extra-bright voice. "Go into the living room and sit down!"

"I won't say no to a nice sit-down," Mel's mum said with a smile, putting down her bag. "But what's going on, Mel?"

Mel took a deep breath. "Well, we're putting on a fashion show for you," she said. "Just here in our living room."

"A fashion show?" Mel's mother frowned. My heart sank.

"Come on, Mum," said Mel encouragingly. "You haven't even seen it yet. Just give us a chance."

"All right, all right." Mel's mother sat down wearily and took off her coat.

I can't help it. I just zoom in on clothes like a moth to a candle. Mel's mum had a good figure. She

44

was tall, and had curves in all the right places. But she was wearing this shapeless black bin-liner thing that clung in all the wrong places. I couldn't help wondering why she didn't wear the jewel-like colours we were about to model up and down the living room any more.

Just then, Lucy poked her head around the corner and pointed the remote at the music system in the living room. The music swelled.

"Welcome to our show, which we have called the New Eighties!" Mel announced from the hallway. "First off, we have Coleen, with a fresh new bite on an old favourite. Take it away!"

Mel's mum's mouth dropped open as I swung in, my hands on my hips.

"That's never my old jacket!" she said.

I don't think she'd ever seen her yellow jacket worn with such va-va-voom before. It was like a mini-dress on me. As well as the patent belt, I'd teamed it with dark green tights and my favourite strappy shoes, not to mention a great pair of gold earrings.

"For your second course," Mel continued, "we have raspberries and cream over chocolate – mmm, take it away Lucy!"

Giggling with embarrassment as she tripped over a pair of shoes that were a bit too big for her, Lucy walked into the living room. Her red and white printed blouse billowed out over a low-slung cowboy belt and Mel's chocolate-coloured jeans.

"My blouse!" Mel's mother gasped. "I'd forgotten what a great pattern that is!"

"And for dessert," Mel said, swinging smoothly into the room in the emerald green dress, "we have peacock pie!" She picked up the peacock pendant and twiddled it around her fingers as her mum laughed in amazement.

46

I had dashed out of the room as soon as I'd finished my turn in the yellow jacket, returning in the shimmery purple trousers and a little purple tee with my favourite orange and silver scarf tied around the middle just as Mel finished twirling the peacock pendant.

Lucy had decided that she would only model one outfit. Now she turned up the volume on the next song, and was singing the words gently in the background as I pirouetted back out to the hallway and Mel bounced in wearing the blue glass earrings and the orange jersey dress over the pair of electric blue trousers.

Mel's mum was shaking her head like she had water in her ears as Mel and I returned one last time, me wearing a full-length red dress and a pirate bandana of pink silk, and Mel in tight orange leggings and a mint-green batwing top. Lucy crooned the last words to the song, and all three of us danced together as the music faded away.

"Well?" Mel asked her mum eagerly, when we had our breath back. "Did you enjoy it, Mum?"

"Unbelievable," her mum said, looking dazed. "All those clothes – you took me right back! I'd forgotten… You updated everything, girls! It all looked so *different*!"

"It's amazing what you can do with a few accessories, Mrs Palmer," I said quickly, and took Mel's hand. "The school fashion show is going to be really good fun – just like tonight! You didn't think we were being objectified, did you?"

"And the clothes are going to be sold for charity," Lucy added. "So it's doing good too."

Mel took a deep breath. "I know you said you'd made up your mind, Mum," she said, "but is there any way you could maybe – unmake it?"

 48

Mel's mum smiled. "You three are impossible," she said. She reached out to touch the beautiful red dress that I was wearing. "How can I resist?" she said at last. "You can do the show, Melanie. But I don't want to see anything tarty or—"

And then she disappeared under a pile of red, pink, mint-green, orange, red, white and chocolate-brown as me, Lucy and Mel all cheered and jumped on top of her.

Four

The sun was blazing down as I jogged to the bus stop the following Monday morning. I knew how the sun was feeling, because I was feeling it too. My favourite lesson first thing, *and* I'd actually enjoyed doing my homework for once! I was feeling pretty confident about my fashion theme, and not even Dave Sheekey making pig faces at me by pressing his nose up against the approaching bus window was going to put me off my stride.

"Good work, Dave," I said as I climbed on board.

"Keep it up and your nose might stay there. Believe me, it would be an improvement."

Dave slid away from the window with a scowl on his face. I felt the world go all slow-mo as Ben slung his arm over the back of his seat and grinned at me as I went past. My excellent morning immediately went stratospheric.

"Drunk your happy juice today?" Mel teased as I sat down with a huge smile plastered all over my face. "You really ought to cut down, Col. Smiling that hard can't be good for your facial muscles."

"Did you do your theme?" Lucy asked anxiously. She was looking at a crumpled piece of paper on her lap. "I did mine on rainbows, but it's not very good."

"I'm sure it'll be fine," I tried to reassure her. I could imagine floaty outfits in all the colours of the rainbow swishing down the catwalk.

"I got my inspiration from our catwalk show,"

said Mel. She waved her piece of paper at me. "Ta-da! New Eighties! What about you, Coleen?"

"Wait and see," I said primly.

"Col!" Lucy wailed. "Tell us!"

But no matter how hard my mates pressed me about my theme, I just smiled and tapped my nose at them. They were practically ready to kill me by the time we got to Miss O'Neill's classroom. And when Miss O'Neill looked around at us all and said, "So, who wants to be the first to argue their theme for our fashion show?" Mel actually pushed me out of my seat.

"Trust Coleen to barge to the front," Summer said in a loud voice.

"Trust Summer to have a voice like a foghorn," I snapped straight back.

Summer glared as Mel and Lucy giggled. Everyone else just looked expectantly at me. And I found that all of a sudden, my mouth had gone dry.

What was my theme? I hadn't even got round to taking my homework out of my bag, and I was stood there in front of everyone like a lemon. Everything drained out of my brain and escaped through my ears like slippery spaghetti.

"Take your time," Miss O'Neill said kindly, seeing that I'd frozen to the spot.

Time! Everything came back into my head just in – well, just in time. And with a rush of relief, I realised that I didn't even need my notes. I'd practised it in front of my bedroom mirror so many times that I could've recited it in my sleep. And so – trying not to think too hard about the horrible combination of high-waisted brown trousers and yellow frilly blouse that Miss O'Neill was wearing today – I began to speak.

It was an amazing feeling, talking to a class full of people when you know they're all listening really hard. Well, Summer and her mates Hannah and Shona were whispering, and all the lads were looking bored, but you don't expect much of boys when it comes to fashion, do you? It helped when a sunbeam shot across the classroom floor in a brilliant stripe of yellow just when I was talking about my ideas for dawn and morning. I could see Mel's eyes misting over and just knew that she was imagining a fabulous sunrise outfit. And, unlike my dad, Miss O'Neill nodded like crazy when I got to my moths idea for dusk.

"And last of all," I finished excitedly, "the blues, blacks and silvers of the midnight sky will sweep down the catwalk, before a tinge of red signals that the new morning is approaching."

Mel and Lucy started clapping. Even Summer clapped – if slow clapping counts.

"Great ideas, Coleen," said Miss O'Neill warmly as

I floated back to my seat. "Let's see if anyone out there can match that. Who's next?"

I couldn't believe some of the rubbish the boys came up with. They had everyone dressed as space explorers / aliens / football players. Mel's eighties idea went down really well until some of the lads started singing old Kylie tracks that drowned out what she was trying to say. To Lucy's horror, three other girls did a rainbow theme – though Lucy's was way the best. And last of all, it was Summer's turn.

"I would like to propose Beach Time: the perfect theme for our fashion show," Summer announced, tossing her blonde hair back over her shoulders.

Beach time? I gawped. That was like – sand and donkeys. Wasn't it?

"Clothes as wild as crashing waves. Crisp linen in gorgeous ice-cream colours. The coolest surf gear for the lads," Summer continued.

The lads stopped whacking each other around the heads with their books and cheered.

"She's going for the lads' votes!" I whispered to the others in dismay.

"Hot bikinis," Summer continued with a smirk, "and cool guys in shades."

There was more whooping from the boys. Mel made sick faces at me.

"Flaming bonfire colours and glamorous beach parties," Summer said. "The sound of the sea in the background, and songs that make you think of summer." She gave a stomach-turning little curtsey. "That's it."

"I hate to say it," Mel muttered as Summer minced back to her seat with a smirk on her face, "but that's a good idea."

"She is sooo annoying!" I said indignantly. I had thought my idea was a winner, but a tiny worm

56

of doubt was starting to chew away my confidence.

"Time for our discussion," said Miss O'Neill, cutting through my thoughts. "I think the first thing we should do is take a vote." She consulted her list. "Who liked Coleen's idea of time?"

There was a decent show of hands. Mel and Lucy loyally stuck both their hands in the air in an attempt to boost numbers. I was pleased that a couple of the cool lads – who usually sat at the back of the class and didn't join in – put their hands up, while Summer and her mates made a great show of sitting firmly on theirs. Predictable, huh?

It was a relief when the space explorers, aliens and footballers sank without a trace. Mel's eighties idea did OK, and so did all the rainbows. Then came the bit I was dreading.

"And last of all," said Miss O'Neill. "What did everyone think of Summer's beach theme?"

My heart plummeted as loads of hands flew up. Lucy and Mel looked sympathetically at me.

"Summer's not allowed to vote for herself, Miss!" I shouted, peering over at Summer's table where she was sneakily waving both hands in the air behind Shona.

"Thank you, Coleen," said Miss O'Neill drily. "I had noticed."

"*Sneak*," Summer hissed at me, narrowing her eyes so much that she looked like a Siamese cat.

"*Cheat*," I hissed back.

Summer and I were so busy shooting evils at each other that we almost missed Miss O'Neill's verdict.

"It looks like we have joint winners," Miss O'Neill was saying. "Coleen and Summer both achieved eight votes each – even accounting for a bit of double-handed voting."

Mel and Lucy blushed. So did Hannah and Shona.

58

"There's no *way* I'm working with her, Miss," Summer snarled, looking at me.

Miss O'Neill looked irritated for the first time. "Enough, Summer," she said sharply. "We're all going to work *together* here. Can I suggest a compromise?"

I don't mean to be nasty, but Miss O'Neill and fashionable ideas go together like chocolate and gravy. I could feel my gorgeous time theme slipping away.

"What kind of compromise, Miss?" I said dully.

"Mixing your two ideas, so we have a day and a night at the beach," Miss O'Neill said, to my total and utter surprise. "Cool sea-spray mornings, boiling beach afternoons, bonfire colours for early evening and a show of glamorous beach-party outfits to take us through to midnight. The set designers can create seascapes for both day and night, and the band can sing – I don't know – some songs by the Beach Boys?"

Half the class groaned at the Beach Boys bit, and Summer rolled her eyes at the fact that she'd be sharing the limelight with me. Me? I was sat there like a stunned kipper. Miss O'Neill's suggestion was brilliant.

"All those in favour?" Miss O'Neill glanced around the room.

Nearly everyone stuck their hands in the air. Miss O'Neill scribbled something briskly on her clipboard. "Good," she said. "So that's decided, then. Next step – writing to the town boutiques to ask if they would donate suitable outfits to be auctioned for charity at the end of the show. Can everyone make a list, please, of the shops you want to invite to take part."

A burst of excited chatter broke out across the room. Even the lads stopped larking about and looked enthusiastic, imagining themselves dressed up like surfer dudes.

"That's perfect!" Lucy said, clutching my arm.

"There are loads of fantastic beach songs we can do!"

"I want a sunrise-coloured outfit," Mel decided. "There's a brilliant orange and yellow kaftan dress in the window of that shop by Woollies. We should write to them for definite."

"I know exactly what I want," I announced. "There's this gorgeous midnight-blue top that I saw in the window of Forever Summer at the weekend. It just needs a bit of magic to make it perfect!"

As you've probably guessed, Forever Summer is Summer's dad's boutique. Summer boasts that her dad named it after her. If he'd really done that, he would've named it Spoilt Princess.

The others made faces at the mention of Forever Summer.

"Assuming Summer's dad donates that top to the show – and remember, Coleen, his stuff is really expensive. I can't see Summer letting you wear it without putting up a fight," Mel said after a moment. "Can you?"

For pretty much the first time that day, my megawatt mood dimmed right down. "OK," I said, trying to shake off the uneasy feeling that was suddenly swamping me. "Assuming Mr Collins donates it, Miss O'Neill will decide who wears it. Not Summer Collins."

I glanced across at Summer. She was staring right at me. With a nasty swoop in my stomach, I had a feeling that she'd just heard every word.

Five

"**D**id you hear what I just said, Coleen?" Mum's words brought me back down to earth with a bump. "Can you move your stuff off the table and lay it for tea?"

"Oh Mum," I groaned. "Can't Em do it? I'm just finishing my maths homework."

"I did it yesterday," Em answered quickly.

"I'll do it tomorrow and the day after," I pleaded.

"And the day after that?" asked Em.

"All right, you've got a deal," I said, sighing.

I peered down at the page of fractions. If I could just finish this last one… There! Quickly I collected up the mass of papers and went into the other room where my plans for the midnight-blue top from Mr Collins' boutique lay on the couch. The first thing I decided was that it needed two rows of tiny pearl buttons down the front. But by Tuesday, I'd decided that buttons was my worst idea ever.

"I'll look like a calculator," I declared as I sat down for tea, scrumpling up my design and lobbing it across the room. "Anyway, I don't suppose I'd be allowed to do anything to the top anyway. We're not meant to use needles on the clothes, cut them up or do anything that'll change them so they can't be changed back again."

Rascal chased my balled-up design hopefully across the floor, skidded on Mum's freshly washed tiles and bumped his nose into the bin. Em snorted with laughter.

"I hope you're laughing at Rascal and not at me," I grumbled, taking up a fresh piece of paper. "This is harder than it looks, you know. It's got to be a *glamorous* beach outfit, like the type of thing movie stars wear. We're talking South California, not Southport."

"You don't even know if Mr Collins will donate it, Coleen," Mum pointed out, fiddling with the stove until the friendly sound of blopping baked beans filled the air. "And why do you want it so badly if you're going to change it anyway?"

I thought about trying to describe to Mum the gorgeousness of silk jersey – the super-cool fabric that the top was made out of. Silk jersey was slippery and fine, and it hung in fabulous folds if you wore it right. I also wanted the top because it was totally plain: a blank canvas for my fashion experiments. But there are some things that no amount of talking can ever totally explain.

"Maybe I could scoop it up at the sides somehow," I murmured, sketching again. "With a silver camisole peeping through—"

"Beans, beans are good for your heart," sang Dad, coming into the kitchen with wet hair from the shower he always took after work. He's a plasterer, and he's always covered in white dust at the end of the day. "The more you eat, the more you—"

With perfect timing, the sound of our toast popping up drowned out the rest. I put my drawing of the midnight-blue top on the side, my head still full of beach thoughts. Rascal lay on my feet as we ate, his whiskers tickling my ankles. I munched my tea as daintily as I could, pinching up my face to look gorgeous and haughty and imagining I was hanging out somewhere on a beach in California.

"Who are you trying to be, love?" Dad said, eyeing me over a forkful of beans. "Angelina never-very Jolie?"

"I don't suppose movie stars eat beans for their tea much," Mum said.

"Poor things," said Em.

And I guess my little sister had a point.

By the time the next drama lesson came around, my plans for the midnight-blue top had changed again.

"I'm going to make a silver sash to tie around the waist," I told Mel and Lucy as we filed into the classroom. "Showing off your waist is a big thing at the moment. There's some fabric I've seen that would look brilliant. I—"

"Thank you, Coleen," Miss O'Neill called. "Time to concentrate, I think."

Summer sniggered as I subsided.

"Last week we made a list of possible shops that we could approach for our fashion," said Miss

O'Neill, handing out sheets of headed paper with the Hartley High address on. "Today we are going to be writing to them."

"I can just ask my dad, Miss," said Summer loftily. "He'll give us loads of stuff. Why do I have to bother writing to anyone else?"

"Everyone gets a letter," Miss O'Neill continued, ignoring Summer. "It's good manners. The list is on the board, and your name is beside the shop I want you to write to."

To Mel's delight, she got the shop with the orange and yellow kaftan she wanted. Lucy had to write to the big department store at the top of town. And I got Tuckers, a fairly cool men's outfitters that had just opened in the town centre.

But you know when you have an idea that gets into your head and takes root? I was like that with the midnight-blue top, and I was determined to do all I could to get it.

"You're writing that fast," Lucy commented, looking over from her corner of the table.

"I want to write to Mr Collins as well," I explained, my hand flying over the page as I explained to Tuckers the importance of our project and how it would give them a chance to introduce themselves to everyone in Hartley and show us all the great stuff they sold. "Just to make sure he includes that top."

"You're obsessed, Coleen!" Mel sighed, shaking her head.

"Maybe I am," I said, finishing my letter with a flourish and grabbing my second, *totally* more important piece of writing paper, "but this is the coolest project we've ever had. Mum and Dad and all our friends will be at the show and I just want to do my best."

Walking down to the park on Wednesday afternoon to meet my dad and little sister after school, I just *happened* to take a detour down Foxton Row. It was a dead glamorous shopping street full of quirky fashion boutiques, and I loved checking out the window displays for the latest looks. Forever Summer stood on the corner, its big plate-glass window glinting in the afternoon sun. I checked my watch. I still had five minutes before I had to meet Dad and Em. Five long, luxurious minutes to stare through the window at what I couldn't help thinking of as My Top.

At first glance, it wasn't much. Most people's eyes would drift over it, caught by the silver minidress that sparkled in the centre of the window display instead. The silver dress was an example of

70

something hideous that got window-time because it came with a big flashy label. In my opinion, it looked like a deflated helium balloon. No, the midnight-blue jersey top was much more interesting. I couldn't see the label because – unlike the silver dress, which had a screaming logo sewn on its sleeve – it was tucked round the back of the mannequin's neck. I sighed with pleasure, and tilted my head so I could catch the top's delicate shimmer. Once I'd given it my magic touch, it would go *perfectly* with my old white cut-offs and a pair of sparkly-flip flops, which I still had to persuade Mum to buy for me. I would be the last model to take to the catwalk. There would be a standing ovation. I'd see Mum and Dad in the front row, with proud looks on their faces. I'd catch a glimpse of Ben's admiring grin from further back. The bidding would go crazy. And the top would be sold to someone super-stylish...

Ten pounds? Who'll give me ten pounds for this unique piece of fashion history? Ten pounds, thank you, Madam! Twelve pounds – fourteen – sixteen – slow down, everyone, I can't count this sea of waving hands – eighteen pounds forty-seven... going... going... gone to our model and designer, Coleen herself!

I sighed. The top would probably go for more than £18.47, but since that was all the money I had in the world, my daydream would have to do.

Somehow, five minutes had slipped into ten. Tearing myself from the window, I raced down Foxton Row. Dad would kill me if I was late for Em's match.

My little sister plays football for our local under-eights team on Wednesdays in the park. I've never fancied playing myself. Still, I do the big-sis thing and support from the sidelines, while Dad trots up and down playing ref. Sometimes he gets a bit carried away, and forgets that it's only a bunch of seven and eight year-olds. He yells and jumps and blows his whistle like he's pounding the sidelines at Old Trafford.

I zoomed around the corner and raced into the park. Out of nowhere, a small, fluffy black poodle came trotting out of the hedge, straight across my path. I leaped and twisted into the air like something out of *Strictly Come Dancing* (I wish!), missing the poodle by about a millimetre of fluff.

"Where did *you* come from?" I panted, putting my hands on my hips and staring down at the fluffball. "I could've squashed you flat."

The poodle blinked at me with a pair of very shiny black eyes. It wasn't wearing a lead, but it had a fancy tartan collar on with a dangly silver name-tag.

"Gucci?" I said in amazement, peering at the name tag. "Your name is *Gucci*?"

Don't get me wrong: Gucci is an amazing fashion

label. But who in their right mind would give that name to a dog?

A tall blond man came running down the path towards me, an empty lead dangling from his hand. He looked familiar, but I couldn't remember where I'd seen him before.

"Gucci!" he called anxiously. "Come here, you bad boy!"

Gucci panted happily at me as I held his collar, waiting for his owner to reach us.

"Thank you," gasped the man, seizing the poodle's collar and snapping the lead back on. "You bad Gucci poochie," he said as the dog licked his fingers.

I was starting to get the giggles. Gucci was bad. But Gucci poochie was worse.

"Oochie coochie, Gucci," said the owner, tickling the poodle under the chin.

74

When I laugh, I snort. Honest. I sound like a pig. Dad always teases me about it, which of course makes me snort even louder. I clapped a hand over my nose. It's the only way to stop the snorting once it gets going.

"Thank you, young lady," said the man. "My daughter would've killed me if Gucci had got out of the park. He's terrible at escaping. I think we should've called him Houdini."

It was no good. The snort was about to escape, just like Gucci. But then my urge to laugh vanished, like it had never been there. Summer Collins was slouching along the path towards us, scowling with boredom.

"Dad," she whined. "Can we go home now? My feet hurt."

Cogs whirred in my brain. Dad? *Mr Collins!* The blond man was Summer's father, and the owner of Forever Summer! Suddenly a poodle called Gucci made sense.

"It was no trouble, Mr Collins," I said, composing my face.

Summer recognised me. Her scowl turned as sour as month-old milk.

"Hello, Summer," I said cheerfully, like we were best mates.

"Do you two know each other?" asked Mr Collins in surprise.

"We're in the same class," I said. "I'm Coleen."

I held my breath. Would he know who I was?

"Coleen? Hey, I received your letter this morning," said Mr Collins, his face clearing. "You're doing the fashion show with Summer, aren't you?"

"Come on, Dad," Summer mumbled, tugging at Mr Collins' sleeve.

I was determined not to let Mr Collins out of my sight until I knew whether there was any chance of getting the top for the show. "Yes, I am," I said

earnestly. "And having some clothes from your store would really make our show special. Like the blue top I mentioned."

"I'll certainly think about including it," Mr Collins said with a smile. "Nice to meet you, Coleen. And thanks again for catching Gucci."

Summer gave me a super-fake smile. Then, as her dad turned away, she dropped the act. "If you think you're getting that top, you'd better think again," she hissed.

I wagged my finger at her. "Now, Summer," I said, "remember what Miss O'Neill said about working together?"

I tell you, if lasers could shoot from human eyes, I would've been a smoking pile of dust on the path.

By the time I got to the park, they were well into the

first half and Em was already covered in mud. She beamed from ear to ear when she saw me arrive. My little sis can be so cute, even dressed in shorts, footie boots and a liberal spattering of mud.

I suddenly felt really warm inside. I'd done all I could to get the top. Now I'd just have to wait. But I like to think I was one step closer to persuading Mr Collins – and to seriously annoying stuck-up Summer. Erm… Gucci the dog? As if!

Six

It was the following Monday, and we were back in our drama class. We'd all been having this long discussion about what music to choose for the show, and things had got really heated. It had already been decided that the show would feature a mixture of recorded tracks and live songs from the band, but it was nearly impossible to decide on anything more than that. So after some really fierce arguing – Justin Timberlake v. Razorlight... The Killers v. Rhianna – we ended up with a mixture of old and new tracks covering stuff like Lily Allen, Pink, the Beach Boys and the Beatles. Some of them were a bit obvious maybe, and totally ancient, but the oldies were easy and perfect for the band to perform. The trickier stuff was saved for the recorded tracks, which would play off the computer that Mr Ratnasinghe the IT teacher (known as Mr Rat for short) was going to set up especially for the show.

But even though we'd taken votes, at least one person in the room still wasn't happy.

"What's up, Lu?" I said. "You look like you've seen a ghost."

Lucy had been in a huddle with the other band members ever since the list of music had been fixed, and had just come back to our table. She swallowed and pointed at a song in the middle of her list. "The band wants me to sing solo on that one," she said, showing us.

"Brilliant!" Mel squealed. "You'll be fantastic, Lucy."

Lucy hung her head so her hair fell over her face. When she does that, it means she wishes she could disappear for real. "I don't want to be lead singer," she mumbled. "I just want to sing backing vocals."

"Have you told the others?" I asked.

Lucy shook her head. "They were all dead keen for me to do it."

"There you go, then," I said. "They think you can do it. We think you can do it. What's the problem?"

"What if I sing it really badly?" Lucy asked unhappily.

I snorted. "You? Sing badly? That's like saying Wayne Rooney can't kick a ball."

Miss O'Neill clapped her hands for silence, and we all turned to face the front.

"We've heard back from two stores this week," Miss O'Neill said, holding up two letters. "And it's good news from both." She glanced over at me. "Your letter to Tuckers worked a treat, Coleen. They're offering us five men's outfits."

A big cheer went up. I gave my best royal wave.

"The only problem," Miss O'Neill continued, "is that we don't have any boys among our models. Would someone please offer to change roles and help us to model these clothes? Or I'll be faced with the embarrassment of writing to Tuckers and having to turn down their kind offer."

The boys muttered among themselves and stared at the floor. You could tell there was no way any of them was going to do modelling. One lad got up and minced about the room, to howls of laughter from his mates. Miss O'Neill watched with her arms folded, looking unimpressed.

I don't get boys sometimes. They think everything's sad, apart from football and guitars. They won't get involved with anything.

"Andrew?" said Miss O'Neill hopefully. "What about you?"

Andrew was a beanpole of a lad, all ears and ginger hair. He wasn't exactly model material, apart from being tall. But he usually did what he was told.

Not this time. Instead, he went so red that he almost turned purple, folded his arms and shook his head. The other lads yelled with laughter, like the thought of Andrew Donovan modelling anything but Airfix aeroplanes was the craziest idea in the world.

"Andrew!" they chanted. "Andrew! Andrew! Andrew!"

Through the din, the bell started to ring. Miss O'Neill couldn't make herself heard above the cheering, and the class collapsed around us like a house of cards.

"Poor Miss O'Neill," said Mel, hurrying down the corridor with me and Lucy as the whole of Hartley High flowed from one classroom to the next like a big blue and grey river. "She'll never get the boys to join in."

"We've got to get some lads to model those clothes, or our show's going to end up looking really sad," I said, shaking my head in frustration.

As we were passing the dining hall, a group of older boys came down the corridor towards us. It was Lucy's brother Ben and his mates Dave and Ali. My hand flew up to pat my hair into place. Then I started grinning. I couldn't help it. It was like my mouth was a torch, and I had to beam my teeth in Ben Hanratty's direction.

"All right, Luce?" Ben said to his sister as he passed us.

Lucy was still deep in her worried-lead-singer thoughts, and didn't notice. But I noticed something all right.

"Ben just nodded hello at me," I said breathlessly to Mel, watching Ben's back disappearing in the crowd.

"I think he was agreeing with something Dave Sheekey had just whispered in his ear," Mel said, ever practical.

Ignoring her, I floated away on one of my little dream clouds. First, that smile on the bus the other day. Now this! Maybe at last Ben Hanratty was starting to see me as someone other than just his little sister's mate…

And then an almost-more-glorious thought struck me. I grabbed Mel's arm.

"Ben and his mates could model for our show!" I gasped.

Mel burst out laughing. Then she stopped, because I had my totally serious face on.

"No way," Mel said. "Coleen! Are you mad? Year Ten lads helping a bunch of Year Eight kids by dressing up and waltzing down a catwalk?"

"Well, it's worth a try, isn't it?" I shrugged.

I glanced at Lucy, ready to run my idea past her. But it was clear from her face that she was still worrying about her singing. Now wasn't a good time to bring this up. Deep in thought, I moved on down the corridor. How could I persuade Lucy's brother to help us when just the sight of him made me blush? I could feel my cheeks starting to glow at the thought of asking him. This could be tricky…

Two lads from our class – the beanpole red-haired Andrew Donovan and his best mate Daniel Thorburn agreed to model a couple of outfits the following week, but only after some hardcore persuasion (and probably threats) from Miss O'Neill. The plan was that the lads would get changed a couple of times and model all the outfits that way. I still thought getting Ben and his mates in on

the act was a better idea, but we had to start somewhere. After all, there were just two weeks left until the show.

All the clothes that had come in were now hanging on a rail in the drama room supplies cupboard. Unlike Andrew and Daniel, who were scowling so hard you could've cleaned a draining board with their faces, the girls kept going into the cupboard to see the clothes and whispering amongst themselves about who was going to wear what. There was no sign of anything from Forever Summer yet. Although I was starting to get worried, I was determined not to lose hope.

I hadn't seen much of Lucy lately because she'd been rehearsing with the rest of the show's band during lunch breaks. She spent most of our drama classes with the other musicians as well.

"In about two minutes," Lucy mumbled, "Suzanne

– she's playing guitar – wants us to do *Here Comes The Sun* for the class."

"Brilliant!" I said enthusiastically. "Isn't that the one where you do your solo?"

Lucy looked close to tears. She nodded. Then she went even paler as Miss O'Neill clapped her hands for our attention.

"I'm delighted to say that our show band will now perform…" she began. But before she had finished, Lucy bolted out of the room.

"I'll go, Miss!" I said, jumping up and racing after my friend as Miss O'Neill stopped mid-sentence with a look of shock on her face.

Lucy was slumped against the corridor wall as I ran outside.

"I can't do it, Col," she said. "Everyone will laugh at me."

Lucy's nerves were worse than I thought. I put my

arm around her. "What's the song again?" I asked.

Lucy gave a tearful sniff. "*Here Comes The Sun.*"

"Looks more like *Here Comes the Snot* to me," I said, pulling a hankie from my pocket and giving it to Lucy to wipe her nose. "I love that one. My dad always sings it when he's watering the garden."

Lucy noticed that I was trying to guide her back into the drama room. She dug her heels in. "I'm not doing it," she said. "I've made up my mind."

Miss O'Neill put her head out of the door. "Everything OK?" she asked.

"Sorry, Miss," said Lucy, looking at Miss O'Neill with watery eyes. "Please don't make me sing today."

"Don't worry, Lucy," said Miss O'Neill kindly, holding open the door so me and Lucy could go back in. "There's still plenty of time. We'll hear one of the other songs instead."

Two weeks isn't plenty of time, I thought anxiously.

Now, on top of the whole how-can-I-get-Ben-to-model thing and the maybe/maybe-not Forever Summer top, there was another problem. If Lucy couldn't perform her song in front of the class, how was she going to do it in front of the whole school in just a fortnight's time?

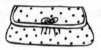

Me and Mel were extra gentle with Lucy at break. I knew there was no point mentioning the singing just then. But as she kept on crying and hiding behind her hair, I decided that a bit of shock therapy might be just what she needed. It was time to mention my Big Plan.

"I think we should ask Ben and his mates to model for our show," I declared.

The effect on Lucy was incredible. She went from being all red-eyed and quivery to gawping and laughing in two seconds flat.

"That's what I did too," Mel said, shaking her head. "But Coleen's determined."

"Totally," I said. I put my extra-determined face on, the one Dad always describes as my constipated look.

"There's *no way* he'll agree to it, Col," said Lucy, putting her hands in the air, "but there's no harm in asking, I guess. Why don't you both come round to ours this weekend? Ben's having his mates over for a game of footie in the garden. You can try and ask him then. But if you end up looking stupid, Coleen, it will *so* be your own fault."

Seven

I got up so early on Saturday morning that Mum thought I was ill.

"Are you sure you're OK, Coleen?" she asked, dishcloth in hand, as I bounced into the kitchen at seven-thirty, my hair freshly washed and already done up in my plastic curlers.

"Couldn't be better," I said, pushing Rascal off my chair (his favourite) and helping myself to toast.

"It's a bit cold for shorts today," Mum said, eyeing my outfit. "Don't you think?"

I glanced down at my new shorts. I'd cut them down from an old pair of jeans that morning, and I was planning on edging the frayed leg bits with some purple glittery ribbon I had in my sewing box.

"Chill, Mum," I said. "I'm going to put tights on underneath. I was just checking they were the right length. You can't tell till you put them on, see."

Dad appeared at the kitchen door. He did this comedy stagger thing and leaned against the doorframe. "I'm seeing things," he said. "Water. I need water..." And he passed his hand over his forehead like he'd been tramping through the desert for days.

Em peered around from behind Dad, her eyes all round and surprised. They were both in their tracksuits, ready for their usual Saturday morning footie training.

"I don't see what all the fuss is about," I objected, pouring some juice into a glass. "I'm up just a bit earlier than normal. That's all."

echoed. "Your mum usually has to

covers off you at ten."

I tapped my nose at him. "Stuff to do," I said. "Me and Mel are supposed to be round at Lucy's by eleven, and I want to get ready."

"Three and a half hours should do it," Dad agreed.

And for some reason, everyone laughed.

My stomach was fluttering when me and Mel got off the bus near Lucy's house at eleven. I was pleased with my shorts, and had spent ages deciding whether to put them with black or purple tights. Purple won in the end, because they looked brilliant with my black pumps. A white T-shirt and a black hoodie with a purple drawstring completed the look. My hair had been a disaster when I took the curlers out: I'd looked like Gucci the poodle. So

I'd washed it again and dried it straight. Mel meanwhile had done something totally flamboyant with her hair, fluffing it into a crazy Afro with a red scarf keeping it off her face. She looked great in her red jeans and stripy tee. If we couldn't persuade Ben and his mates to model for us when we looked this good, then there was no hope!

As we got nearer Lucy's house I could hear all this yelling and laughing coming from the back garden. My confidence started oozing away.

"Sounds like the lads are already here," Mel said nervously.

"No problem," I said, trying to sound more confident than I felt as I knocked on the Hanrattys' door. "Let's go and find Lucy first."

"She's in her room." Mrs Hanratty smiled as she nodded her head in the direction of the stairs. We slipped past and hot-footed it up to the landing.

Lucy grinned as we pushed back her door. "All set?" she asked.

"Well, it's now or never," I said, swallowing.

We hurried back downstairs and into the garden. I spotted Ben immediately. He was in goal, laughing and with a huge stripe of mud down his jeans. My stomach did its beach-ball thing. Then I groaned when I saw Dave Sheekey playing keepie-uppies by the patio, while Ali Grover – usually the quietest of Ben's mates – cheered him on.

"I guess we can't have everything," Mel muttered in my ear.

I decided that a confident approach was necessary, took a deep breath and marched down to the grass.

"Hi, Ben!" I said. It came out a bit squeaky, but I figured I was the only one who noticed.

Ben grinned and waved. I grinned back my manic

torch-beam smile. And then Dave Sheekey decided that he'd had enough keepie-uppies, and kicked the ball straight at me.

I panicked, did a half-jump like I was trying to head it, missed, slipped in another puddle that was lurking on the path and landed flat on my bum in a flowerbed. Mel rushed to help me up as the lads burst out laughing. Yup. Even Ben.

You know when you think, can I just die right now and get this over with? Well, this was one of those times. I was totally on fire with embarrassment. The man in the moon could've lit a bonfire from the heat coming off my face. There was a massive streak of mud down my purple tights, and the edging had come away from the hem on my left leg.

"How bad was it?" I said in a low voice as Mel helped me inside.

"On a scale of one to ten?" Mel asked, pushing me

through the open patio door as the lads doubled over out on the lawn. "About eleven and a half."

"Oh Coleen!" Lucy gasped. "Your clothes!"

I don't cry easily, so I was horrified when I felt these hot tears prickling behind my eyeballs. Desperate not to smudge my mascara – Dad's make-up radar doesn't stretch as far as mascara – I sniffed hard and fumbled for a bit of kitchen paper to catch the drips. My outfit was a wreck. I had mud under my fingernails. And now Ben was looking in through the kitchen door.

"You OK?" he asked.

I nodded tragically. I wasn't sure what was worse: Ben seeing me like this or the wriggly lines around his mouth that proved he was still laughing but desperately trying not to show it.

"Take Coleen upstairs, Lucy," said Mrs Hanratty from where she was loading the washing machine.

98

"I'm sure you've got something you can lend her? Bring your clothes down when you've changed, Coleen love. I'll pop them in this wash for you. And if you leave your shoes by the door, I'm sure Dave can clean them up. Can't you, Dave?"

There was a glint in Mrs Hanratty's eyes which told me she'd seen everything that had just happened. It's amazing how much she can look like a sabre-toothed tiger when she wants to. Dave skulked into the kitchen and scooped up my pumps like an obedient little puppy.

Smiling weakly at Mrs Hanratty, I trailed out of the kitchen and followed Lucy and Mel upstairs.

Lucy's bedroom is not at all what you'd expect – not for such a girly girl. One wall is painted black, and the rest are a really hot pink. The pink walls have loads of shelves on them, and the black wall has Lucy's massive collection of music and movie posters. They look brilliant, and always make me dream of Hollywood.

Strains of *Here Comes The Sun* were floating out of Lucy's computer speakers when we shut the door behind us. It sounded like our mate had been practising her solo when we arrived. It reminded me of Lucy's nerves about the show, and I hoped she was feeling braver about it now. She is such a brilliant singer – I just wish she knew it. Why was nothing ever simple?

"Take your pick, Coleen," said Lucy, flinging open her wardrobe.

I stared at the rows of pastel blouses, jeans and plain jumpers inside the wardrobe. Hmm. Some fashion magic was badly needed here.

Lucy was looking at me anxiously. "I'm sorry it's all a bit boring," she said.

"There's no such thing as boring," I said. "It's just how you mix it up."

♡ 100 ♡
♡

Lucy pulled armfuls of clothes on to her bed and stood back, looking embarrassed.

"This is like a makeover," Mel said in excitement, plunging her hands into the pile of clothes and pulling out a couple of tees that matched her red jeans.

My spirits were rising. I pounced on a stretchy little navy-blue dress that I instantly knew would look great over my white T-shirt – which, somehow, was still mudless.

"You're not serious," Lucy said when I held the dress up to myself. "I wore that to my aunt's wedding when I was like, nine!"

"Then, it was a dress," I said. "Now, it's a tunic top. Perfect."

Mel flopped back on the bed amongst all the clothes and grinned at Lucy's expression. I pulled off my muddy tights, shorts and hoodie. Then I wriggled into the dress and checked myself out in the mirror.

"That's mad," said Mel approvingly.

"And way too short," Lucy pointed out, grinning.

I glanced through her trousers. Most of them were too long for my little legs. But then I spotted a white pair of leggings. They probably reached just past Lucy's knees, but on me they almost hit my ankles.

"Ta-da," I said, giving a twirl. "What do you think?"

"Mum won't believe she's seeing that dress again," said Lucy, shaking her head at me.

"Good choice, Col." Mel nodded approvingly.

The flowerbed nightmare was almost forgotten. And Ben had been kind of sweet about it, hadn't he? But we still hadn't broached the subject of the fashion show.

"Right," I declared. "Remember our plan?"

"Yes indeedy," said Mel.

"Go for it!" said Lucy confidently.

"Just say it like we practised," I told them as we

made our way back downstairs. "We'll have Dave Sheekey eating out of our hands by the end."

"I always thought Dave looked like a horse," Lucy giggled.

The lads were all inside now, sitting round the kitchen table with packets of crisps and glasses of Coke. Dave broke into the theme from *Match of the Day* when we came into the kitchen, but that was no surprise.

"Thanks for cleaning my shoes, Dave," I said sweetly, taking my scrubbed-up pumps and slipping them on. "It's great having you at my feet where you belong."

Ben and Ali laughed, and Dave made a squishy kind of face that meant one-nil to me. Mel nudged me in the back. If we were going to pull this off, I needed to be nice to *all* the lads. Even Dave.

"That's never Lucy's gear you're wearing, Coleen."

I almost fell over. Ben was speaking straight at me.

"Um, yeah, yeah, it is, mmm…" said Coleen, winner of the Silvertongue Award 2008.

"It looks totally different," said Ben. "Good one."

Mel nudged me fiercely in the back again. We had to move on with Phase One of our plan. I held down the beach-ball and cleared my throat.

"Exercise suits you lads," I began, looking round at the table. "You don't look bad for it – quite toned, in fact."

"Yeah, not bad at all," Mel added.

Ben rolled his eyes and Dave did a few strong-man impressions. Ali wriggled a bit, but you could tell he was pleased.

"Anyway," Lucy said, "we're going next door to watch a DVD for a school project we're doing. See ya."

I casually waved *Gary Lineker's Action Replay* in the air. I'd borrowed it off Em, with the promise that I'd buy her a bar of chocolate that afternoon.

If our plan worked, I was going to make it two.

Satisfied that we'd baited the trap, me, Lucy and Mel tripped back out of the kitchen and into the living room. Now all we had to do was wait.

"Quick," I hissed, handing Mel a glossy mag as Lucy slipped the footie DVD into the player. Lucy's mum loves fashion mags, and there were half a dozen on the living-room coffee table. "They'll be in in a minute."

We flung ourselves down on the couch. Mel opened her magazine. I grabbed a pen and pad to complete the 'project' look. And, just as the music started up, Ben and his two mates wandered in.

Boys are so predictable, aren't they? Phase Two of our plan was about to begin.

Eight

"Reckon you need all the footie lessons you can get, Coleen," said Dave, flumping down on the couch beside me. "Tell me the part about offside again?"

I bit down the retort that rose to my lips and tried to focus on the Plan. Everyone settled down as the DVD began.

Mel ruffled the pages of her mag really loudly.

"Oi," said Dave. "I'm trying to listen."

"Aren't you supposed to be watching this?" Ben said, his eyes glued to the screen.

"In a minute," Mel said, just like we'd practised. "There's just this brilliant page of male fashion models I want to look at in my magazine."

On cue, Lucy and I both jumped up and rushed over to Mel.

"Give us a look," said Lucy.

"Check out that leather jacket," I said loudly, looking sideways at the lads to see if any of this was sinking in. "It makes him look really buff."

"I like that white shirt," said Lucy. She glanced at the screen, where David Beckham was belting a ball up the pitch. "David Beckham wears one just like that," she improvised.

Ben glanced round at this.

"Rio Ferdinand too," I added, laying it on a bit. "Those footie lads really know how to look good, don't they?"

"Give us that." Dave pulled the mag from Mel's hands.

Trying not to grin, I made a show of grabbing it back again. It was time for the killer blow.

"You'd be great as a model, Ben," I said, as casually as I could.

"Oh, Ben doesn't care about fashion," said Lucy at once. "He could wear a bedsheet and think it looked OK."

"Wait up," said Ben, looking annoyed. "I take pride in my appearance, thanks very much."

"Yeah, right," Lucy said. "You've got like, two T-shirts in your wardrobe, and they've got holes all over them. Admit it, Ben. Fashion just isn't your thing."

"Just because I don't have loads of stuff, doesn't mean I'm not into fashion," Ben argued. He snatched the magazine off Dave and peered at the pictures we'd been looking at.

Mel winked at me. Everything was going perfectly.

108

"So prove it," said Lucy, folding her arms and staring at her brother. "Let Coleen style you. You can choose the clothes, and Coleen will add the finishing touches. Then we'll judge whether you can look fashionable or not."

Dave burst out laughing and jabbed Ben in the ribs. "Oooh!" he crowed. "Ben's going to be a mo-del!"

Ben scowled. "Shut up Dave," he said. "OK, I'll prove it. But only if you guys do it too."

Dave stopped laughing immediately. Ali went a bit pale. We glanced anxiously at each other. This had never been part of the plan. There was a horrible pause as Ben's mates frowned. I didn't see a problem with styling all three of them – so long as they all agreed. *Please*, I prayed to myself. This bit was crucial to the Big Plan. *I'll do anything. I'll get three bars of chocolate for Em. I'll tidy my room. I'll even sort my sock drawer. Please…*

Dave clapped his arms around Ali and Ben. "Show us the way to the catwalk then, girls," he said.

I let out the breath that I didn't even know I was holding. It was hard not to cheer out loud.

"We'll stay here and be the judges," said Lucy, looking at Mel who nodded.

"We'll be back in twenty minutes," I said, trying not to jump up and down. "And you won't believe your eyes!"

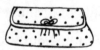

There was no time to feel nervous about being upstairs with Ben Hanratty and his mates. I marched towards Ben's room and flung open the door, with Ben and the others following me.

"Phew," I said, fanning my nose at the pong of old socks and teenage boy. "Don't you ever open a window in here?"

110

Embarrassed, Ben opened it immediately. Then he opened his wardrobe while I braced myself for its contents.

It was worse than I had imagined. Four old shirts hung on coat hangers. A bundle of old trackies and jeans lay in a blue heap on the floor. And a tangle of hairy jumpers in seven shades of brown huddled on the shelves like a bunch of really embarrassed rabbits.

Ben reached into the depths of his cupboard while Dave and Ali poked around in his music collection. "This is my favourite T-shirt," he said, holding it up. "It's fashionable, isn't it?"

It wasn't bad: white with a faded red and black picture on the front that was supposed to be a kind of warning sign like the ones you see at electrical substations. It was also the dirtiest T-shirt I'd ever seen.

"What's it warning you about?" I said, taking the

T-shirt between my fingers like it was going to explode. "Health and hygiene?"

I was stumped. Five minutes had already passed. The lads were going to get bored really quickly. And then our Plan was dead in the water.

Mr Hanratty put his head around the door. "Everyone all right in here?" he asked.

Lucy's dad looked just like Ben, but older. He was wearing a really nice light blue jumper and a pair of decent jeans. Shame that Ben didn't have the same sense of style, I thought with a sigh.

Then inspiration struck. Call me crazy, but I was desperate.

"Mr Hanratty?" I said, as Lucy's dad started to withdraw. "Do you think we could borrow some of your clothes?"

112

Twenty minutes later, I peeped around the living-room door. "Ready?" I asked Lucy and Mel.

"Bring it on," Mel declared.

Borrowing Mr Hanratty's clothes had been a brilliant move. It had just been a matter of totally ignoring the lads' yells of protest. They'd stopped protesting pretty quickly when they saw how hot they looked.

Ben was wearing a white shirt, open to his waist with his favourite T-shirt showing through underneath. He had on one of his dad's jackets with the sleeves rolled up to his elbows. On the bottom half, he was wearing the cleanest pair of jeans that I could find in his wardrobe, and trainers at the bottom which I'd fixed with different coloured laces. Ali was in a black jumper and Mr Hanratty's suit trousers, a very shiny pair of Mr Hanratty's work shoes peeping out at the bottom and a trilby hat on his head. And Dave –

well. All I can say is that it had nothing to do with me.

"Whoo," said Dave, pirouetting into the room in one of Lucy's mum's best dresses. "Look at mee-hee!"

Lucy and Mel cheered and clapped. Ben broke into a slow grin, and opened his jacket to show off his shirt. Ali even did a bit of a shoe shuffle, looking like Justin Timberlake struggling to stay upright on an ice rink.

"Whoo!" Dave yelled, cantering across the room and lifting his skirts to point his toes.

"Brilliant!" Lucy gasped, gawping at her brother. "You too, Ali."

"And you look surprisingly good in a dress, Dave!" Mel added, laughing her head off.

Ben looked made up as he tweaked the collar of his dad's jacket and stuck his hands in his pockets. I'd never seen Ali looking so confident either. Dave bounced up to the couch and did a somersault on

the cushions, ending up on the floor in a pile of frills with his boxers flashing at everyone. As the whole room fell about, I knew it was now or never.

"How about modelling for our end-of-term show, then?" I asked. "The lads in our class refuse to wear the brilliant stuff we've got. You'd be total heroes if you helped us out."

Ben grabbed Ali's trilby and grinned out from underneath the brim. "Sure," he said. "So long as Dave gets to wear a dress."

Miss O'Neill was chuffed to bits when we told her about Ben and his mates helping us with the modelling – and she wasn't the only one. Andrew Donovan slid up to me and Mel in the dinner queue that week and mumbled something that sounded like: "Cheers, you've saved my life," before scurrying off

115

to join an equally relieved-looking Daniel Thorburn.

With our three new male models in the bag, everything else at last started falling into place. The sets were almost finished. The comperes were almost word-perfect on the introductions they were doing for each section of the show. The clothes from Forever Summer still hadn't come, but were supposed to be arriving in time for our last drama class. Posters were stuck up all over the school, and halfway around town as well. Our charity was the local children's hospice: they were sending someone to talk to the audience at the start of the show, and we were all really hoping that we'd make a mint for them.

The only serious fly in the ointment was Lucy, who still hadn't performed her solo for the class. She'd been practising loads and was determined not to pull out. But she was still stuggling to overcome her nerves. Even Miss O'Neill was getting impatient.

"You've got to face an audience some time," Miss O'Neill said, each time Lucy refused to sing for the class.

"I'll be fine at the dress rehearsal," Lucy mumbled. "Honest, Miss, I really want to do it. It's just not right yet."

Lucy's musician mates insisted that she was sounding great in the private rehearsals they were doing. So Miss O'Neill sighed each time, and just looked a bit more worried. It seemed like we all just had to trust Lucy on this one.

I stopped in my tracks as we came into the drama class in our final week before the show. The midnight-blue jersey top from Forever Summer trembled enticingly on its padded hanger on the clothes rail, and next to it – the dead-helium-balloon silver dress.

Let me explain something here. Clothes had been arriving for weeks now. Most of the girls had already asked Miss O'Neill if they could wear this, that or the other, and most of it was finalised. I'd decided to hold off on asking Miss O'Neill about an outfit until something came in from Forever Summer. There was a chance that I wasn't going to get the top anyway, but it was a chance I had decided to take. Needless to say, Summer Collins had done exactly the same thing. We'd been prowling around each other for ages now, like deadly scorpions playing musical chairs. And finally, it looked like the music was about to stop.

I raced straight up to Miss O'Neill. "Please Miss, can I wear that?" I asked, pointing with a trembling finger at the blue top. "I wrote specially to Mr Collins to ask him if he'd put it in the show. I've been waiting and waiting and—"

"Summer's already expressed an interest in the top," Miss O'Neill interrupted. "How about the silver dress instead?"

I gawped in horror at Summer. Smiling smugly,

118

she waved at me with the tips of her fingers. This couldn't be happening!

I turned back to Miss O'Neill. "You haven't decided for definite yet, though, have you, Miss?" I said in desperation.

"Well," Miss O'Neill began.

"But that top would look horrible on Summer, Miss!" I wailed.

Summer zoomed across the room to join in the discussion.

"I've been waiting for ages for that top too, Miss," she simpered. "I asked my dad especially if he could send it in, just so I could wear it in the show—"

"She's lying," I shouted. "*I'm* the one who—"

"Enough!" Miss O'Neill shouted, waving her arms in the air.

We both ground to a halt. Everyone fell silent and swung round to stare at us.

 119

"Let's take a vote," Miss O'Neill said, passing her hand over her forehead like she always does when she's stressed. "You both model each garment, and the whole class will decide who should wear what."

I reached for the top, but Summer snatched it off me and ran behind the big painted beachscape scenes that were stood up against the back wall of the classroom. Slowly I took the silver dress and followed her. What if the class decided against me? What if *I had to actually wear the helium balloon?*

Nine

For once, Summer and I were silent as we got changed. This was too important for bickering. To my horror, the blue top looked quite good on Summer, even with her grey school skirt on the bottom. I slid into the crinkly silver folds of the dress, wincing at the scratchy feel of the fabric. I was *so* not into the whole logo-crazy astronaut look.

Then I saw Summer looking hard at the silver dress. Something that looked a bit like envy was flickering across her eyes. It dawned on me that she actually *liked* it, and this whole thing was just about getting one over on me!

As I was processing this thought, Summer pushed past me and walked out from behind the screens. There was a round of applause. I could hardly bear the suspense as I inched out from behind the screen and walked up and down the classroom behind Summer. Everyone's eyes were on us. Me and Summer's eyes were everywhere but on each other.

"Next," said Miss O'Neill.

It was as tense as a cowboy shoot-out back behind the screens. Summer and I silently exchanged outfits. I slid into the top, and couldn't help a sigh of pleasure as the silk jersey rippled all cool across my skin. Summer fiddled with the scrunchy silver hem on the dress. Even considering that it was totally disgusting, the dress looked much better with Summer's long legs than it had with my little ones. Then we were

out again, walking up and down like prize penguins.

"Thank you," said Miss O'Neill at last. "Let's take that vote. Who thinks Coleen should get the silver dress?"

I hid my eyes. I wasn't going to try and count the hands.

"And who thinks it looks better on Summer?" Miss O'Neill continued.

I stayed firmly behind my hands. The top wrapped snugly around me, like a big silk hug.

"That's decided then," I heard Miss O'Neill say. "Summer gets the dress and Coleen gets the top."

My legs wobbled under me, but thankfully didn't buckle. I almost couldn't believe it. The top was mine.

"The top looked *so* much better on you than that bit of kitchen foil!" Mel said enthusiastically as she rushed over to give me a hug.

"Summer's welcome to it," Lucy agreed, patting me on the back.

"No one gets one over on me," snarled Summer. "Especially *you*, Coleen. You wait. I'll get you back. You'll see."

The rest of the week picked up speed like a skateboard on a hill. There was still so much to do that I didn't have time to worry about Summer Collins and her nasty little threat. To tell you the truth, I totally forgot about it – which gives you some idea of how busy we all were. The days blurred into one as we spent every second we were out of class doing all the last-minute things that were needed for it to run smoothly on Saturday night. We still had the dress rehearsal on Friday afternoon, and then that was that. Show time!

Even if you weren't in Year Eight, it wasn't hard to work out who was doing what for the show. The set-

painters were the kids permanently covered in yellow and blue paint. The musicians wandered around with frowns of concentration on their faces and humming the same tunes over and over. The models were practising strutting down the corridors (me included). Everyone was excited. You could practically taste it in the air.

And then it was Friday afternoon and school was out. We stood in a huddle outside the hall for our dress rehearsal as all these totally over-excited kids raced past, off to start half-term as fast as they could.

"All right for some," said Andrew Donovan, watching everyone screeching out the gates. He and Daniel Thorburn had been put back on lighting duty for the show, and they were trying really hard not to look too pleased about it.

Miss O'Neill appeared, jingling a set of keys. "Hopefully this won't take too long," she said, unlocking the hall so we could all file inside out of the wind. "We'll just run all the lighting cues, get our models to take a turn down the catwalk in the correct order, and listen to the music as well. Mr Collins has taken the clothes for safekeeping overnight, and will bring them back at six o'clock tomorrow, ready for kick-off at seven."

Mel and I glanced at Lucy. She was looking up for it, standing with the other band members and humming gently under her breath. A great feeling of relief swept over me. Lucy was going to be fine. There was no need to worry.

Even though I'd seen everything a million times during our drama lessons, I couldn't help gasping when I saw the hall. Everything was finished, and it looked unbelievable.

The catwalk stretched from the stage steps right down the middle of the hall. A few cute beachy things

like starfish, seaweed and fish had been painted on it for that extra seaside touch. Huge green, yellow and blue banners hung around the walls. The surfboards, fishing nets and baskets were propped up beside the catwalk as well, plus piles of pebbles and seashells. Up on the stage, a massive white curtain hung down. It was going to swish like the sea behind the models, and a bunch of brilliant lights were going to shine on the curtain and change colour through the show – from pale misty-morning colours through to yellows and blues and bonfire oranges and reds until, last of all, a special filter would scatter stars across the curtain like the night sky.

Mr Rat's computer was all set up, and a couple of the lads were in charge of cueing up the recorded music. The rest was down to the band, who were setting up in a special corner of the stage.

"Good luck, Lucy," I said, giving my mate a massive hug.

"You're going to be the best," Mel added.

Lucy looked pale but determined. She grinned bravely at us and headed across to join the band. I grabbed Mel's hand and pulled her up on to the stage as well. We took our places in the line of models all waiting impatiently behind the curtain.

"Andrew!" Miss O'Neill shouted, peering backstage at the lighting desk where Andrew and Daniel were fiddling with switches. "Are you and Daniel ready? A lot of this stuff will be new to you. Let me know if the instructions aren't clear. The most important thing of all to remember is that you should never have more than three lights on together. Our old lighting rig can't take the current. OK?"

"No problem, Miss," said Andrew, who was peering in confusion at a bunch of switches somewhere near the top of the lighting desk.

"I don't think Andrew Donovan and Daniel

Thorburn could find their own bedroom light switches," said Mel to me in a low voice. "Let alone a switch in the middle of a hundred others."

"Don't worry about them," I said, giving her a push. "Go on. You're in the bonfire part. That's just ahead of me."

As part of the beach-party section, I was going on last – along with Summer Collins, Hannah Davies and...

"All right?"

Ben Hanratty was standing right next to me, grinning. Behind him, Ali Grover and Dave Sheekey stood balancing on the end of the stage, daring each other to stand a bit closer to the edge and not to topple over. Everyone was trying not to goggle at them, like Year Tens helped out Year Eights all the time. Well, most of them were trying not to. Summer, Hannah and Shona were goggling like a tank of tropical fish.

"Hiya!" I said breezily, enjoying every second of being the person that Ben was talking to. *Boing, boing, boing.* My beach-ball was bouncing so hard that I could feel it squeezing up my throat. Mel flipped a wink at me, like she knew exactly how I was feeling.

"Hi there."

Me and Ben both turned round to see Summer fluttering her long black eyelashes at him. And I mean *really* long, and *really* black. No *way* were they for real. She was stood with her hands on her hips and her body swivelled just a bit, like she was a celebrity out on some red carpet instead of a kid in school uniform.

Mel started making a ringing noise like a telephone. "Hello, Hartley High make-up police?" she said into an imaginary handset. "Send a squad car. There's a set of eyelashes here that are totally criminal."

I burst out laughing. Summer flushed angrily.

 130

Then, before things could turn nasty, we heard the first chords of the band's opening number, *Walking on Sunshine*, blasting out across the hall. The rehearsal was underway.

One foot in front of the other. Sway the hips. Don't fall over. I recited my instructions carefully as I shuffled up the line of models, imagining how it would feel to be wearing the midnight-blue top tomorrow night, with the silver belt that I'd made over the weekend. I could feel Summer's eyes boring into my back, but I refused to let her put me off. This was way too important. *One foot in front of the other. Sway the hips. Don't fall—*

There was a bang and the shattering sound of glass. Somebody screamed. Smoke started stealing around us as the band faltered and stopped like a bagpipe running out of air. Miss O'Neill raced through the curtain.

"What happened?" she gasped as everyone coughed and waved their hands in front of their faces.

Andrew Donovan peered sheepishly over the top of the lighting desk. "Was it four lights that shouldn't go on together, Miss?" he asked. "Or three?"

And then the fire alarm went, and it was the end of the shortest dress rehearsal in history.

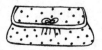

"So you and Mel never got to practise your parts?" Dad asked, frowning over his cup of tea as I explained to everyone back at home what had happened.

I shook my head. "And Lucy hasn't done her song either," I said miserably. "The lights blew out half the electricity in the hall, including all the wires for the band's mikes and instruments. It's going to take them hours to fix it. And the fire brigade came and told us we couldn't go back inside until they'd

132

checked it all, and then we ran out of time, and now everything's a total mess."

"Is the show still going ahead?" Mum said.

I nodded. "So long as they can mend the lights and replace the fuses in time. But there's no way we'll be able to fit in another dress rehearsal."

"Those lads on the lighting desk should be fired," Dad said. "Sounds like they couldn't find a piece of coal in a bag of flour."

I was feeling really wobbly all of a sudden. "It's going to be scary doing it all without a proper rehearsal," I said, chewing my lip. "Not knowing whether we're going to make mistakes, or whether the lighting's going to work for real, or whether Lucy's going to be brave enough to sing her song for the first time to a full hall." I looked up at my family in despair. "What if everything goes wrong, and we all look really stupid?"

"You'll be fine," said Em unexpectedly, looking up from the apple she was busy crunching. "It's like a football match."

"Not *everything* compares to footie, Em," I snapped.

"You can't plan the best matches," Em said between crunches, ignoring me. "They just happen. You've got to have that unpredictable thing, or it's just a load of boring rubbish."

She finished her apple and handed the core to Rascal. Rascal loves apple cores. He gobbled it up like it was steak. We have one seriously weird dog.

"There's no point worrying about it," said Mum in her practical voice. "I'm sure everything will be fine. And we'll love it whatever happens."

Trailing up to my room after tea, I tried to think about the show the way Em had described it. My little sister can be quite wise for a seven-year-old with zero

sense of style and a blinding left foot. Maybe everything *would* be OK after all. *She shimmies... she shoots... she swooshes... she scores... GOOOOAALLL!!* But somehow, I was having a problem believing it.

Coleen, fashion star or fashion flop? Only tomorrow would tell.

Ten

I t was ten to seven on Saturday night, and "Beach Time: The Show" was about to begin.

The place was packed out, and the murmur of voices out in the hall sounded like the rhythmic swooshing of waves against our catwalk. The bust lights had been replaced and the electricity problem sorted. Backstage, there'd been a panic half an hour earlier when Shona Mackinnon's mum had called Miss O'Neill to say that Shona hadn't eaten anything for three days and was now too ill and exhausted to

do the show. Erm, what do you expect from stupid diets like that? But everything else was good to go.

The first models were already wriggling into their outfits: some brilliant whites and greys and palest pink dresses and tops that billowed around exactly like dawn mist – at least, if you put your mind to it.

On the far side of the stage, a group of lads stood around a canister of dry ice with Mrs Matthews, the science teacher, getting ready. When the chords of the intro music started up – a totally weird choice by Mr Rat, by some group called The Grateful Dead – they were going to open the canister and the dry ice was going to billow out across the catwalk and make it all misty and eerie. Music was already pumping out of Mr Rat's speakers, and there was this hubbub out in the dark hall which sounded exciting and scary and wonderful all at the same time.

After a great morning shopping with Mum – we'd

found the most *perfect* pair of sparkly flip-flops to go with the blue top and my white cut-offs – I was more or less back to my old self. Even without a rehearsal, I had decided that I was going to be positive and go with the flow. It wasn't every day that you got the chance to model something as brilliant as my midnight-blue top, and I was determined to make the best of it. Plus, I was standing next to Ben Hanratty, wasn't I?

Just like we'd practised in class, we all stood in the order we were going on in. Ben was modelling his jacket in the beach-party section, like me (and Summer and Hannah too, worse luck), so we were right at the back of the line. Dave and Ali were modelling some surfy gear for the afternoon section, and were stood further up ahead of us. Mel was on for the sunrise part so she was supposed to be near the front – though right now, she was peeping

through the curtains beside me. As there wasn't enough room for everyone to change at the same time, we were supposed to shuffle up the line as each section went on to the catwalk, reach the clothes rail and then get changed around two songs before our entries. I'd come to school in my white cut-offs and flip-flops already.

"There's like, a *thousand* people out there, Coleen," Mel gulped in excitement, still peeping through the curtain. "We're really doing this!"

"I feel sick," Lucy muttered, pacing up and down beside Mel. The words to her song were clutched so tightly in her hand that they were all crumpled and the ink was running over her fingers.

"Throw that bit of paper away, Lucy," I said, peeking over Mel's head at the sea of expectant faces out in the darkness of the hall. Mel's mum was out there – she was wearing the yellow jacket we'd modelled for her at our sleepover! She even had a black belt cinched in around her waist. I felt a rush of total satisfaction that we'd given Mel's mum the courage to wear her cool clothes again. Then I saw my parents and Em sitting near the edge of the catwalk, and my stomach squeezed up all tight and nervous.

"I can't throw my words away. I don't know them yet." Lucy's teeth were actually chattering together.

"You've been singing those words up in your room for weeks, Lucy," said Ben. "You know those words back to front."

"Don't say that," Lucy said, sounding a bit hysterical. "I might sing them that way."

"Five minutes." Miss O'Neill bustled past us, wearing – shock horror – quite a nice dark green dress with a crisscross thing going on over her back. "All dawn and morning models, please be sure to have your outfits on."

"Gotta go," said Mel, and dashed up the line towards the rail and her fabulous orange and yellow dress.

"I *am* going to be sick," Lucy wailed.

A hush fell over the hall. We could all hear someone speaking. It sounded like Mrs Gabbitas, our Head Teacher.

"She's introducing the lady from the hospice," I heard someone saying further up the line.

Lucy had gone as white as chalk. The paper with her words written on it drifted out of her fingers and landed on the stage. She took a step backwards.

"I'm not going on," she said.

Everyone around us stopped dead. I recovered first.

"You've got to, Lucy!" I hissed as fiercely as I could. "The band needs you!"

Lucy burst into tears. "I can't, I feel too nervous," she sobbed.

"But there's nothing to feel nervous about," I said.

"You are totally brilliant. I would love to be able to sing like you."

"Me too," Ben smiled and rubbed his sister's shoulder encouragingly. "With a voice like yours I could even be the lead singer of Take That."

Lucy laughed and looked as though she was starting to feel a little better.

"Here, wear this," I said, reaching over to the clothes rail and grabbing a brooch from Shona Mackinnon's dress. "For luck."

"For luck," Lucy said, tracing the brooch with her fingers.

"Leona Lewis, eat your heart out," I cried.

I could almost see Lucy standing up taller as she thought about what I'd said.

There was a round of applause out in the hall. It sounded as if the hospice lady had stopped speaking. We were seconds away from starting the show.

 142

"We're on, Lucy." Suzanne, the band guitar player stopped beside us, blissfully unaware of the drama.

"Go!" I shouted.

And to my total unspeakable relief, Lucy went.

The applause for the band rippled through the curtains. I turned to head back to my place in the line – and bumped straight into Summer. She looked like some kind of evil light was shining through her. Triumph gleamed in her eyes as she blocked my way.

"What?" I demanded, staring her down.

"Looking forward to your big moment, Coleen?" Summer purred.

"Right now, I'm looking forward to pushing you out of my way," I growled back.

"You're going to look soooo stupid," Summer crowed. "Have you seen your precious top lately?"

And with a silvery laugh, she trotted off to join Hannah Davies at the back of the line.

143

The hippie, misty notes of Mr Rat's Grateful Dead track started swirling out of the speakers. I could smell the dry ice hissing out of the canister. The first speaker was introducing the dawn. Dread grabbed at my guts.

How could I have forgotten Summer's threat?

I spun around and pushed up the line to the clothes rail. Pulling out my top, I stared dumbly at the huge, ragged holes that had been cut into it. Slash marks ran the length of the arms, and the seams at the side had been ripped apart. I knew at once that my silver belt was never going to hold the top together. It was ruined.

The Grateful Dead ended, and the cheery notes of *Walking on Sunshine* started up from the band. The audience cheered. Deaf to it all, I clutched the top and ran.

My brain was whizzing at a million miles an hour.

 144

Everything had been held at Summer's dad's storage place overnight. She must have got hold of the key. Tears sprang to my eyes. I kept running. Shoving past everyone, I leaped down the backstage steps.

"Coleen!" Miss O'Neill ran after me, waving her clipboard at me. "Come back! Where are you going?"

It was a good question. Where *was* I going? My feet had a mind of their own. I flew down empty corridors like something in a nightmare, pushing at classroom doors in a desperate bid to find something – anything…

Textiles room.

I stopped like I had slammed into an invisible wall. The textiles room door was ajar. People had been in and out of it all afternoon, fixing broken buttons and stitching up hems. There had to be something here that I could use.

Strains of the Beach Boys' *Surfin' USA* floated

down the corridor. With a gulp, I realised how fast the show was moving. It had always felt much longer than just forty minutes in rehearsal. Now those precious minutes were melting away. Trying not to think of my family's faces when I didn't make it on to the catwalk in time, I pulled out drawers and tipped them over the floor, muttering invisible apologies to Miss Smith the textiles teacher. Zips, buttons, feathers, rolls of felt. I threw aside Velcro and rolls of black thread, puddles of silky fabric and balls of wool. Seizing on a large bottom drawer, I heaved it open in desperation.

A bunch of multi-coloured ribbons spilt out of the drawer, rolling away gently underneath the desks and cupboards. I fell on my knees and grabbed handfuls of reds, oranges and yellows. *Dawn sky*, I thought feverishly, seizing a nearby pair of scissors and lopping off lengths of bright ribbon, adding purple and pale blue as I went along. I pulled on the top, seized the ends of the ribbons in my teeth, and started wrapping myself up like a parcel. I wound the red ribbon around one arm, and the orange one around the other. The yellow crisscrossed across my stomach and did a decent job of covering up the thumping great hole. That left the blue and the purple. I turned myself like a chicken on a spit, lifting my arms and tucking the ribbons together as best I could. The top was starting to look less like a torn-up dishcloth and more like something you could wear again. At least, I hoped it was. The only mirror that I had was the window in the textiles room door.

The intro to *Here Comes the Sun* had started up. I stopped, my teeth still clamped around the ribbon ends, and listened. Lucy's voice floated down the corridor like an angel's.

Well, at least that's one less thing to worry about, I thought.

And just as I thought it, the ribbon ends fell out of my mouth and I had to start all over again.

I wanted to bawl. I wanted to lie down and yell and bang the floor with my fists. *Summer Collins had won.* But I found one last, limp little bit of pride, and forced myself to take up the dangling ribbon ends again.

Rhianna's *Music of the Sun* was fading out. Now it was the band's last live song. I carried on, desperately trying to tie and tuck the ribbon ends in place to hold my creation together. Forcing myself to concentrate, I tucked the last trailing ribbon end into my trousers and took a deep breath. Not too deep, mind. There was no way I was risking one of my ribbons pinging off again. I gave myself a long, hard look at my reflection in the textiles room door-window. Then, hugging myself just in case any of the

148

ribbons got some funny ideas about working their way loose, I started running back to the stage.

The corridor had never seemed so long. I could hear Nitin Sawhney's *Sunset* fading out. The little intro of *When You Wish Upon a Star* was about to start, when the first twinkling stars would shine on the stage curtains and prepare the way for the beach-party finale. *My* beach-party finale.

I skidded around the last corner and pelted towards the backstage steps. *When You Wish Upon a Star* was fading, and Pink was about to bring the house to their feet.

"Coleen!" Miss O'Neill looked like she was in a state of shock as she saw me racing towards her. "What... your top..."

"Ask Summer Collins, Miss," I shouted, bombing past her. I flew up those steps like my life depended on it. Which it kind of did.

BOOM!

Pink's *Get the Party Started* leaped into life from Mr Rat's speakers. Nearly everyone had been on the stage already, and were now standing around waiting to go back on for the final bow.

"Out the way!" I yelled.

I nearly crashed into Ben, who was just coming off the catwalk. He did this double-take at me – and then grinned so wide that his mouth practically wrapped around the back of his head. If I wasn't sure I looked hot before, I was now!

"Whoo, Coleen!" Mel whooped, clapping like crazy when she saw what I'd done.

Summer minced through the curtain behind Ben, all silvery and hideous and totally smug. And I'll tell you this: if smugness made a noise when it fell off someone's face, it would make the most satisfying *scrunch* you ever heard.

I blew Summer a massive raspberry. And laughing with delight at the total look of shock on her face, I burst through the curtains, leaping down the steps in one go with my ribbons flying behind me. The show was almost over. But Coleen, Style Queen's fabulous fashion career had only just begun...

You will need:

★ An old T-shirt

★ Pretty ribbon, lace or sequins

★ A pretty button or bead

★ Sharp scissors

★ A needle and thread in a

similar colour to the ribbon

PLEASE TAKE CARE WITH BOTH
THE NEEDLE AND THE SCISSORS!

Step 1

Take the strip of ribbon
or sequins and wrap it
around the hem of your
T-shirt until the ends
meet. Cut it so the ends
overlap by about 1.5 c.m.
Do the same around the
neck and sleeves.

Step 2

Carefully thread your
needle and tie a knot in
the end of the thread.

Step 3

Stitch the top edge of the
ribbon/lace to the hem of your
T-shirt, using tiny stitches, so
the thread hardly shows. When you
reach the end, fold the ends under
and stitch them carefully into place
so the frayed ends don't show. Do the
same around the neck and sleeves.

Step 4

With the remaining ribbon, tie a bow and stitch it firmly at the knot so it stays in place.

Step 5

Grab your pretty button or bead and sew it, with the bow, to the shoulder of your top, so that the button covers the knot of the bow.

VOILÀ!

Your scruffy old T-shirt is now a unique party top!

If bows are not your style, here are some other ideas...

★ Twist the ribbon into shapes or letters
   and sew them on to your top.

★ Find a cool patch or funky logo to sew or iron on.

★ Buy some fabric pens or paint (look out for the
   super-cool glitter pens) and draw your own designs.

OUT NOW!

Dress to Impress

Having a confidence crisis? Don't dare
wear that cute little mini-dress? Then
maybe I can help. I'm Coleen and I love
fashion, friends and having fun.

My best mate Lucy has got a hot date
this weekend and I'm going to transform
her style from drab to fab!

HarperCollins *Children's Books*